D1266434

ANOTHER EYE-POPPING MYSTERY!

SCOOBY-DOO!

LIKE, KEEP A SHARP EYE, SCOOB! THE PHANTOM COULD BE--

WHAT?

THE PHANTOM OF THE OPAL!

PAUL KUPPERBERG WRITER   ROBERTO BARRIOS PENCILLER
HORACIO OTTOLINI INKER   PAT BROSSEAU LETTERER
HEROIC AGE COLORIST   HARVEY RICHARDS EDITOR
VINCENT DEPORTER COVER ARTIST

Spotlight

visit us at www.abdopublishing.com

Reinforced library bound edition published in 2012 by Spotlight, a division of the ABDO Group, 8000 West 78th Street, Edina, Minnesota 55439. Spotlight produces high-quality reinforced library bound editions for schools and libraries. Published by agreement with Warner Bros.—A Time Warner Company. The stories, characters, and incidents mentioned are entirely fictional. All rights reserved. Used under authorization.

Printed in the United States of America, Melrose Park, Illinois.
052011
092011
 This book contains at least 10% recycled materials.

Library of Congress Cataloging-in-Publication Data

Kupperberg, Paul.
  Scooby-Doo in The phantom of the Opal! / writer, Paul Kupperberg ; penciller, Roberto Barrios. -- Reinforced library bound ed.
     p. cm. -- (Scooby-Doo graphic novels)
  ISBN 978-1-59961-924-8
  1. Graphic novels. I. Scooby-Doo (Television program) II. Title.
III. Title: Phantom of the Opal!
  PZ7.7.K87Scm 2011
  741.5'973--dc22

                                2011001373

All Spotlight books are reinforced library bindings
and manufactured in the United States of America.

SCOOBY-DOO!
Table of Contents

THE PHANTOM OF THE OPAL! 4

Car-Tastrophe 16

THE PHANTOM OF THE OPAL!

PAUL KUPPERBERG WRITER   ROBERTO BARRIOS PENCILLER
HORACIO OTTOLINI INKER   PAT BROSSEAU LETTERER
HEROIC AGE COLORIST   HARVEY RICHARDS EDITOR
VINCENT DEPORTER COVER ARTIST

YOU'RE LISTENING TO "CAR CHAT" ON NATIONAL PEOPLE'S RADIO, WITH CLING AND CLANG, THE THUNK-IT BROTHERS. IF YOU'RE HAVING A PROBLEM WITH YOUR CAR, OR NEED SOME REPAIR ADVICE, GIVE US A CALL AT 1-555-CAR CHAT.

WELCOME TO CAR CHAT. YOU'RE ON THE AIR...

THIS IS FREDDIE.

WHERE ARE YOU CALLING FROM, FREDDIE?

UH, I'M OUTSIDE A CRUMBLING, SPOOKY HOUSE ON A STREET LINED WITH MENACING DEAD TREES.

Car-Tastrophe

IT SOUNDS LIKE MY BROTHER'S HOUSE. BWA-HA-HA-HA-HA! LET ME TAKE A LOOK OUTSIDE THE WINDOW AND SEE IF I CAN SEE YOU. HA-HA-HA-HA-HA-HA.

WHAT SEEMS TO BE THE PROBLEM, FREDDIE?

John Rozum - writer
Matt I. Jenkins - artist
Rob Clark Jr. - letterer
Heroic Age - colors
Harvey Richards - editor

CAMBRIDGE, MASSACHUSETTS.
TWO MONTHS LATER...

WELCOME TO "CAR CHAT." YOU'RE ON THE AIR.

NOT FOR MUCH LONGER...

THAT'S WHAT ALL THE PEOPLE WITH SHOWS ON NATIONAL PEOPLE'S RADIO HAVE BEEN WISHING FOR YEARS. BWA-HA-HA-HA-HA!

WHO ARE WE TALKING TO? WITH THAT DEEP, OMINOUS-SOUNDING VOICE, I HOPE YOU'RE NOT MY WIFE ASKING ME TO PICK UP MILK ON THE WAY HOME. HA-HA-HA-HA!

I GUESS MY BROTHER CAN'T GET ENOUGH OF SLEEPING ON THE COT OUT IN HIS GARAGE. BWA-HA-HA-HA.

I AM THE PHANTOM OF THE AIR.

I DRIVE A HEARSE BUILT FOR TWO PASSENGERS. THE PROBLEM IS RIGHT NOW THE HEARSE IS EMPTY.

YOU TWO WILL FIX THIS.

IF OUR PAL FREDDIE IS OUT THERE LISTENING RIGHT NOW, AND DOESN'T HAVE A FLAT TIRE OR ANYTHING...

"...WE WOULD REALLY APPRECIATE IT IF YOU COULD COME HELP US OUT FOR A CHANGE."

YOU CAME IN THAT?! YOU'RE BRAVER THAN I THOUGHT.

I'M JUST KIDDING AROUND. MY BROTHER AND I ARE REALLY GLAD YOU CAME.

THOUGH IT TOOK YOU LONG ENOUGH. HA-HA-HA-HA.

I'M TIM, ALSO KNOWN AS "CLING." THAT DOOFUS OVER THERE IS MY BROTHER ROY, ALSO KNOWN AS "CLANG."

DON'T TELL ME. LET ME GUESS. ONE OF YOU TWO IS FREDDIE. I'D GUESS THE DOG...

I THINK THE MYSTERY MACHINE IS THE DOG--HAH-HA-HA, OR AT LEAST A LEMON.

...SINCE IT SOUNDS LIKE YOU HANDLE YOUR VAN WITH NO OPPOSABLE THUMBS, BWA-HA--

ACTUALLY, I'M FREDDIE.

I ADMIT, I DON'T HAVE MUCH LUCK WITH THE MYSTERY MACHINE, BUT I MORE THAN MAKE UP FOR IT WITH MY MYSTERY-SOLVING ABILITIES.

YOUR MYSTERY-SOLVING ABILITIES. WHAT ARE WE? CHOPPED LIVER?

I'M VELMA. TELL US ABOUT YOUR PHANTOM PROBLEM.

IT ALL BEGAN WITH THAT ONE WACKO PHONE CALL. THEN THINGS STARTED GETTING WEIRD, AND FRANKLY A LITTLE DANGEROUS.

HERE'S A BROADCAST OF A RECENT SHOW.

SO WHAT YOU'RE SAYING IS THAT YOUR RIGHT FRONT WHEEL SEEMS TO BE TILTED AT AN ANGLE, AND WOBBLES WHEN IT TURNS?

THAT'S NOTHING TO WORRY ABOUT. JUST CHANGE YOUR WINDSHIELD-WASHER FLUID AND YOU SHOULD SEE THAT PROBLEM GO AWAY IN NO TIME.

THAT'S OBVIOUSLY, OR WE HOPE IT'S OBVIOUS, NOT THE RIGHT ANSWER.

THE WHEEL SITUATION IS ACTUALLY VERY DANGEROUS. WHAT WE ACTUALLY RECORDED WAS...

THAT'S VERY DANGEROUS. IF I WERE YOU I WOULDN'T EVEN DRIVE IT TO A REPAIR CENTER, I'D HAVE IT TOWED...

THE BIT ABOUT THE WINDSHIELD-WASHER FLUID WAS AN ANSWER WE GAVE TO A DIFFERENT PROBLEM ON ONE OF OUR SHOWS FROM A FEW YEARS AGO.

SOMEONE JAMMED OUR OWN TRANSMISSION AND BROADCAST THAT OLD ANSWER INSTEAD.

SOMEONE COULD HAVE BEEN SERIOUSLY HURT!

IT'S MADE SOME LISTENERS ANGRY, AS WELL AS OUR PRODUCERS. WE'RE WAITING FOR THE LAWSUITS TO COME POURING IN.

AND YOU THINK IT WAS THIS PHANTOM OF THE AIR?

THERE HAVE BEEN OTHER THINGS TOO.

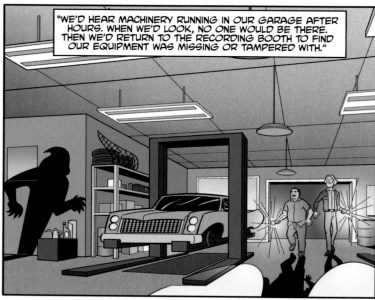

"WE'D HEAR MACHINERY RUNNING IN OUR GARAGE AFTER HOURS. WHEN WE'D LOOK, NO ONE WOULD BE THERE. THEN WE'D RETURN TO THE RECORDING BOOTH TO FIND OUR EQUIPMENT WAS MISSING OR TAMPERED WITH."

HAVE YOU EVER SEEN THE PHANTOM?

ONLY ONCE.

I HOPE NEVER TO SEE IT AGAIN.

⋛ULP⋜

OKAY, GANG. WE'VE GOT SOME WORK TO DO NOW.

PERFECT. SHAGGY, GO BRING ME THAT NET. SCOOBY, GRAB THAT GREASE GUN...

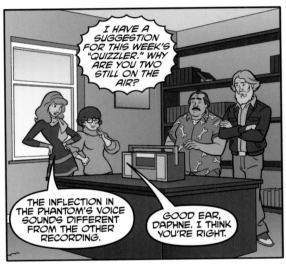

I HAVE A SUGGESTION FOR THIS WEEK'S "QUIZZLER." WHY ARE YOU TWO STILL ON THE AIR?

THE INFLECTION IN THE PHANTOM'S VOICE SOUNDS DIFFERENT FROM THE OTHER RECORDING.

GOOD EAR, DAPHNE. I THINK YOU'RE RIGHT.

TELL ME. WHO HAS ACCESS TO RECORDINGS OF YOUR PREVIOUS SHOWS?

WELL, OUR LOYAL LISTENERS, OF COURSE.

BOTH OF THEM. HA-HA-HA-HA

OURSELVES. ANYONE WITH ACCESS TO THE NATIONAL PEOPLE'S RADIO ARCHIVES, MEANING ANYONE WHO WORKS THERE.

I HATE TO SAY IT, LADIES, BUT WE GO ON THE AIR IN FIVE MINUTES.

WOW! YOU GUYS HAVE A VAN, TOO. IS THAT FOR WHEN YOU TAKE YOUR SHOW ON THE ROAD?

NO WAY! HA-HA-HA. YOU SHOULD SEE OUR BUDGET.

I WONDER WHAT THAT'S DOING THERE.

HMM. I'VE GOT A PLAN. TIM, ROY, BROADCAST YOUR SHOW AS IF NOTHING'S WRONG.

CALL THE POLICE AND REPORT AN ILLEGALLY PARKED VAN OUTSIDE THE STUDIO.

SINCE YOU TWO BUFFOONS HAVE FAILED TO HEED MY WARNINGS, I SHALL COME TO YOU IN PERSON.

WAIT, I KNOW THAT VOICE. THAT'S NO PHANTOM...

THAT'S *KARL CASTLE!* ONE OF NATIONAL PEOPLE'S RADIO'S MOST CHERISHED PERSONALITIES.

BUT WHY?

I'LL TELL YOU WHY.

KARL AND I, AND EVERY OTHER HARD-WORKING, SERIOUS MEMBER OF THE NATIONAL PEOPLE'S RADIO STAFF, WANT TO GO DEAF WHENEVER WE HEAR THE WORDS "NATIONAL PEOPLE'S RADIO" ATTACHED TO YOUR SHOW FULL OF CRASS AND JUVENILE HUMOR.

TERRI GRASS, HOST OF "FRESH BREATH" IS ALSO THE PHANTOM? I'M SHOCKED.

SHE AND MR. CASTLE USED THE TRANSMITTING ANTENNA ON TOP OF THE VAN TO JAM YOUR SIGNAL AND TO BROADCAST IN PORTIONS OF YOUR OLD SHOWS.

"THEY USED SOUND EQUIPMENT TO MAKE THEIR VOICES SOUND MORE OMINOUS WHEN THEY CALLED IN."

ROY, TIM, I HAVE ANOTHER BIT OF CAR TROUBLE I COULD USE SOME HELP WITH...

OH, NO. THEY'RE TICKETING THE WRONG VAN!

SORRY, PAL. WHEN IT COMES TO TRAFFIC TICKETS, YOU'RE ON YOUR OWN.

THE END